||||||| D0571585

Brianna

Godparents - Christine
José - Da Silva

October 27, 2002

Praise God from whom all blessings flow!

BISHOP THOMAS KEN

ISBN 0-8499-7768-1

Library of Congress Control Number: 2001132127

Printed in China

01 02 03 04 05 LEO 5 4 3 2 1

THOMAS KINKADE

Blessings

Tommy NELSON

Thomas Nelson, Inc.
Nashville

God bless all those that I love;
God bless all those that love me;
God bless all those that love those that I love,
And all those that love those that love me.

From an old NEW ENGLAND SAMPLER

Thank You, Lord, for giving me
A happy, caring family.
Thank You for the friends I meet;
And for neighbors down the street
But most of all, dear Lord above,
I thank You for Your precious love.

UNKNOWN

Dear Lord, I'd like to pray
for all the people that I love,
but who live far away.
Tonight with them my thoughts I share.
Please keep them in your loving care,
Each night and every day.

TRADITIONAL

God bless us every one!

CHARLES DICKENS

"Tiny Tim's Prayer"

If we love each other, God lives in us.

1 JOHN 4:12

Thanks to you, kind Father
For my daily bread,
For my home and playthings,
For my cozy bed.

Mother, father, dear ones—
Bless them while I pray:
May I try to help them,
Cheerfully obey.

CHARLES HEALING

All good gifts around us
Are sent from heaven above;
Then thank the Lord,
      O thank the Lord,
For all his love.

MATTHIAS CLAUDIUS

The Lord is good to me,
and so I thank the Lord.
For giving me the things I need:
the sun, the rain, and the apple seed!
The Lord is good to me.

TRADITIONAL

If you have plenty, be not greedy,
But share it with the poor and needy:
If you have a little, take good care
To give the little birds a share.

TRADITIONAL

God bless the field and bless the furrow,
Stream and branch and rabbit burrow,

Bless the sun and bless the sleet,
Bless the lane and bless the street,

Bless the minnow, bless the whale,
Bless the rainbow and the hail,

Bless the nest and bless the leaf,
Bless the righteous and the thief,

Bless the wing and bless the fin,
Bless the air I travel in,

Bless the earth and bless the sea,
God bless you and God bless me.

AN ENGLISH PRAYER (Excerpt)

O Lord Jesus Christ, . . .
help us to be very kind to all animals and our pets.
May we remember that you will one day
ask us if we have been good to them.
Bless us as we take care of them; for your sake. Amen.

UNKNOWN

I will praise you, Lord, with all my heart.
I will tell all the miracles you have done.

PSALM 9:1

North and South and East and West,
  May your holy name be blessed;
  Everywhere beneath the sun,
  As in heaven, your will be done.

WILLIAM CANTON (Adapted)

O Father of goodness,
We thank you each one
For happiness, healthiness,
Friendship and fun,
For good things we think of
And good things we do,
And all that is beautiful,
Loving and true.

PRAYER FROM FRANCE

Two little eyes to look to God;

Two little ears to hear his word;

Two little feet to walk in his ways;

Two little lips to sing his praise;

Two little hands to do his will

And one little heart to love him still.

TRADITIONAL from Wales

All for You, dear God.
  Everything I do,
  Or think,
  Or say
  The whole day long.
Help me to be good.

UNKNOWN

Lord, teach me all that I should know;
In grace and wisdom I may grow;
The more I learn to do Your will,
The better may I love You still.

ISAAC WATTS (Adapted)

Lord, teach me what you want me to do.

PSALM 86:11

God makes our home a house of joy,
Where love and peace are given;
It is the dearest place on earth,
The nearest place to Heaven.

JOHN MARTIN

"Bless My Home"

Lord, behold our family
here assembled. We thank You
for this place in which we dwell,
for the love that unites us,
for the peace accorded us this day,
for the hope with which we expect
the morrow; for the health,
the work, the food,
and the bright skies
that make our lives delightful;
for our friends in all parts
of the earth. Amen.

ROBERT LOUIS STEVENSON

God bless the master of this house,
God bless the mistress too,
And all the little children
That round the table go.

UNKNOWN

God bless our home.

TRADITIONAL

May the love of God our Father
Be in all our homes today:
May the love of the Lord Jesus
Keep our hearts and minds always:
May his loving Holy Spirit
Guide and bless the ones I love,
Father, mother, brothers, sisters,
Keep them safely in his love.

UNKNOWN

Children, obey your parents the way the Lord wants.
This is the right thing to do.

EPHESIANS 6:1–2

Bless, O Lord Jesus, my parents,
And all who love me and take care of me.
Make me loving to them,
Polite and obedient, helpful and kind.
Amen.

UNKNOWN

Bless all parents in their children, and
all children in their parents.

CHRISTINA ROSSETTI

Father, we thank You for the night,
And for the pleasant morning light,
For rest and food and loving care,
And all that makes the day so fair.
Help us to do the things we should,
To be to others kind and good;
In all we do and all we say,
To grow more loving every day.

UNKNOWN

The Lord is my shepherd.
I have everything I need.
He gives me rest in green pastures.
He leads me to calm water.
He gives me new strength.
For the good of his name,
he leads me on paths that are right.
Even if I walk
through a very dark valley,
I will not be afraid
because you are with me.
Your rod and your walking stick
comfort me.
You prepare a meal for me
in front of my enemies.
You pour oil on my head.
You give me more than I can hold.
Surely your goodness and love
will be with me all my life.
And I will live in the house
of the Lord forever.

PSALM 23:1–6

Joy comes in the morning.

PSALM 30:5

For this new morning and its light,
Father, we thank You;
For rest and shelter of the night,
Father, we thank You;
For health and food, for love and friends,
For every gift your goodness sends,
We thank you, gracious Lord.

RALPH WALDO EMERSON

"United States" (Adapted)

My Father, for another night
Of quiet sleep and rest,
For all the joy of morning light,
Your holy name be blessed.

HENRY WILLIAM BAKER (Adapted)

Through the night your angels kept
Watch beside me while I slept;
Now the dark has gone away;
Thank you, Lord, for this new day.

WILLIAM CANTON (Adapted)

For flowers that bloom about our feet,
Father, we thank thee.
For tender grass so fresh, so sweet,
Father, we thank thee.
For song of bird and hum of bee,
For all things fair we hear or see,
Father in heaven, we thank thee.

For blue of stream and blue of sky,
Father, we thank thee.
For pleasant shade of branches high,
Father, we thank thee.
For fragrant air and cooling breeze,
For the beauty of the blooming trees,
Father in heaven, we thank thee.

For this new morning with its light,
Father, we thank thee.
For rest and shelter of the night,
Father, we thank thee.
For health and food, for love and friends,
For everything thy goodness sends,
Father in heaven, we thank thee.

RALPH WALDO EMERSON

May the Lord bless you and keep you.
May the Lord show you his kindness.
May he have mercy on you.
May the Lord watch over you
and give you peace.

NUMBERS 6:24–26

For God loved the world so much
that he gave his only Son.
God gave his Son so that whoever believes in him
may not be lost, but have eternal life.

Thank the Lord because he is good.

His love continues forever.

I CHRONICLES 16:34

Index of Paintings